Junk

Robin Klein

Illustrated by Rolf Heimann

Hodder
Children's
Books

a division of Hodder Headline plc

Text copyright © 1983 Robin Klein
Illustrations copyright © 1983 Rolf Heimann

First published in hardback by Oxford University Press in 1983
First published in Australia and New Zealand in 1994
by Hodder Headline Australia Pty Limited

First published in Great Britain in 1996
by Hodder Children's Books

A Catalogue record for this book is available from the British
Library

ISBN 0 340 65125 3

Typeset by Avon Dataset Ltd, Bidford-on-Avon, Warks.

Printed and bound in Great Britain by
Cox & Wyman Ltd, Reading, Berks

Hodder Children's Books
a division of Hodder Headline plc
338 Euston Road
London NW1 3BH

One

Mandy and Irene and Con Vaskelis and Splinter were in the same grade at school and lived in the same block of flats in Meldrum Crescent. The flats would have been much nicer with balconies, or a decent-sized backyard. There was no room at all to do interesting things, such as taking a bicycle apart, or inviting all your friends around for water-melon and a squirt with the hose on hot summer days.

As well as this hardship, the children had to endure Mr Acland for a grade teacher. Each Thursday morning in his class, someone would have to stand out in front and deliver a ten minute lecture.

They had to choose their own topic. Mr Acland yelled like a rodeo rider if they began any sentence with 'er'. Irene was bashful to the point of being invisible, but Mr Acland didn't accept that as an excuse.

'It's your turn to give a talk tomorrow, Irene,' he said. 'What's the topic? You should have one ready in advance. What's it to be, girl? Quick, quick, stop mumbling, I haven't got all day!' And Irene said, 'Incubating chickens,' in a faint voice, because that was the first thing that popped into her numb and terrified mind.

On the way home from school she started hiccuping violently. She always did that when she was nervous. The hiccups sounded so dramatic and intense that Mandy, Con and Splinter rendered immediate first aid. They sat her down on the bottom step and put a brown paper bag over her head. But Irene went on hiccuping, and it sounded even more alarming with the bag as an amplifier.

Mr Felsenthal stuck his head out of his

3

ground floor flat and told Irene to shut up because he was trying to listen to the 3.45 from Moonee Valley racetrack. So they took Irene into Mandy's flat and gave her a drink of cold tea out of the opposite side of a cup. When that didn't work, they ran her up and down all the stairs between the ground floor and the first floor. Mrs Cooper came out of her first floor flat and told them off because her husband was sleeping to be ready for night shift.

So they took Irene up to the second floor and told her to sing the Crunchmallow TV ad back to front holding her breath. Irene was too self-conscious to sing on her own, so they all did. Mrs Carinani opened her front door and told them to go somewhere else and sing. She was working out her Tattslotto numbers to a very complicated system, and needed peace and quiet.

So Splinter collected his skateboard from his flat and they went back outside into Meldrum Crescent. Splinter's board was a smart fibreglass one with cadillac wheels, decorated with dozens of stick-on labels. He had managed to get such an expensive board by saving up two hundred and fifty gift vouchers from tea packets. He hadn't drunk all that tea himself, his mother worked in the canteen at the hospital.

'A spin round the block might get rid of hiccups,' Mandy said, but Irene was scared of getting on even a stationary skateboard. Mandy coaxed her feet on to it with many tactful, encouraging words, and held one of her arms. Con held the other, and Splinter bent down and pushed the board from behind. Irene kept her balance but she hiccuped loudly the whole length of Meldrum Crescent, past the printing works and the Lebanese restaurant and the milk bar and the group of houses at the end of the crescent.

'It didn't work!' she hiccuped crossly, and got off and leaned against a garden gate.

'You didn't do it fast enough to have any effect,' Mandy said sternly. 'You're supposed to go like Splinter.' Splinter whizzed magnificently to the fire hydrant and back. The little cadillac wheels made a beautiful whirring clatter, like milk bottles being loaded into a crate, or a far-away steam train chattering through a tunnel, or millions of briquettes slithering down a chute at an open cut mine.

'The only thing that cures hiccups is a good fright,' said Con.

'*What the devil are you kids doing making that racket hey kids these days only think of their own amusement I've got a good mind to go and complain to your parents the very idea aren't you the same kids I already told off yesterday for chalking arrows all over the footpath you need a good belting the lot of you and you girl yes you with the plaits what do you mean leaning against my fence like that blocking the sunlight from my dahlias eh speak up?!!*'

Irene sprang away from Mr Drake's

fence, and up. It seemed to Con and Mandy and Splinter that she stayed frozen up in the air with her heels dangling for several seconds, but when she landed, she didn't have hiccups anymore.

Mr Drake glowered over his front fence, and Mandy thought that his face looked just like one of the carved stone faces on Easter Island. She wondered curiously how someone with a sour, pernickety face could manage to grow such glorious dahlias.

'I suppose you thought I'd already left for my holiday and you could tear around and make as much noise as you liked,' Mr Drake said angrily. 'You'd just better not try hullabalooing up and down the street in my presence, or in my absence, either!'

'But there's nowhere else to skateboard,' Con said. 'Not now they went and put the freeway through.'

'There's that park over there,' Mr Drake said. 'If you want to waste your time playing, you get over in that park and do it.'

Two

The park opposite wasn't really grand enough to be called a park. It was just a sandwich-shaped wedge of lawn squeezed in between the Kozisnooze Slumberwear factory and a site where a new service station was being built. It had a railing fence around it and a sign which said, 'The Beatrice Binker Reserve'.

It was too small for a game of football or a game of anything. There were no slides or swings, not even a tree. Just grass. Occasionally someone from the Council came and mowed the grass, but Mandy and Con and Irene and Splinter wished they wouldn't. The Beatrice Binker

Reserve would have been more exciting if it had grown into a small, private, triangular jungle.

'You can't skateboard on grass,' Con said.

'That's the trouble with kids these days never happy when I was a kid I had to get cows in feed chickens and walk a hundred and forty-seven kilometres to school and back you kids ought to be darn grateful someone donated a nice bit of land for a reserve I never had time to play when I was a boy you just keep over in that reserve and don't let me catch you making a din in this crescent again or else!'

Mr Drake glared so fiercely that they scuttled across the street to the Beatrice Binker Reserve. They sat down in the middle of it and tried to make their faces look pleased and grateful. Mr Drake stayed in his front yard and scowled over at them like a totem pole. At least he had cured Irene's hiccups with his loud, fierce voice and his Easter Island face.

'I've got to think up my speech for

tomorrow,' she said dismally. She looked as though she would start bawling. Her face went pink and she put the end of her plait into her mouth and bit it emotionally. Mandy had been trying for years to cure her of being so weepy and embarrassing them all in public places by bursting into tears for such things as a Highland pipe band marching down the street.

'Now cut that out, Irene,' she said briskly. 'You haven't got time to cry. If you can't give a talk about incubating chickens, you'll have to think of something else.'

'I can't think of anything.'

'Air pollution, training guide dogs, parachute jumping, Aboriginal legends.'

Irene shook her head.

'Paddle steamers along the Murray

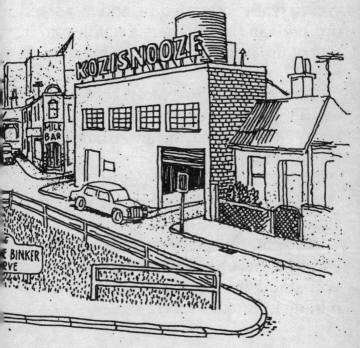

River, advertising on television, Eskimos, how to make very nice Christmas decorations out of balloons and string and a bit of glue and grated carrot.'

But Irene didn't want to give a talk on any of those things. 'I don't want to give a talk at all,' she said.

'Giving a talk is nothing,' said Mandy. 'All you have to do is pick something you're really interested in, and just stand up there and chat. There's nothing to it. Hurry up, Irene, what's your topic going to be?'

Irene thought privately that Mandy would make a very good matron for a large city hospital, or an admiral, or a league football coach.

'We're waiting,' said Mandy.

'Medieval castles, then,' Irene said sulkily.

'All right. All you've got to do is pretend we're Mr Acland and the whole class, and you stand up there and give us a ten minute lecture.'

But Irene looked horribly ill at ease. She scuffled gym shoe patterns into the dusty grass of the Beatrice Binker Reserve, cleared her throat and swallowed each nervous word as soon as she thought of it.

'Say the first thing about castles that comes into your head,' said Mandy.

'Big thick knitting needles,' said Irene.

'That's got nothing at all to do with medieval castles,' Mandy said severely.

'It has so. The first thing that came into my mind was chain armour, and it always looked knitted in pictures.'

'I'm sure knights didn't knit their armour. I saw Camelot when it was on TV and I certainly can't imagine Sir Lancelot sitting around knitting.'

'He must have,' Irene said stubbornly. 'Chain mail armour always looks just like wrong-side knitting. And they didn't have factories like the Kozisnooze Slumberwear in those days, so they must have done it by hand.'

'It's still not enough for your ten minute lecture. What else are you going to talk about?'

Irene made an intricate rose window in the dust, composed of twelve gym shoe prints with the heels radiating from a central point. It took a long time to make.

'Irene!' said Mandy.

'I know as much about medieval castles as I do about incubating chickens,' said Irene.

'I know how to fix that,' said Mandy.

Three

Their local library was wonderful. You could borrow posters and cassettes and magazines as well as books. And there weren't any bossy signs ordering you to shush. You were allowed to talk if you did it quietly and away from the section where the students were working. Mandy looked up castles in the subject index and they went to the shelf number. They found a book with photographs of all the famous castles in Britain, and another book called *Heraldry*, which had lovely bright pictures and information about coats of arms. Irene wanted to find out about knitted armour, but there didn't seem to be anything that looked like a knitting pattern in either of the books.

Then they helped Splinter choose some books for his mother. Because of her job at the hospital canteen, she didn't get very many chances to go to the library and choose books herself. 'Your mum's not interested in motorbike racing,' Mandy said. 'You're only trying to use her card and get out extra books for yourself.' So Splinter put that book back and chose another called *The Night Visitors: Tales to Chill Your Blood*, which had a picture of a vampire on the cover.

After that, they each played a game of chess with Con, who was very good at it though he didn't show off about winning every single time. He just looked modest and apologetic and pointed out that he was hopeless at Scrabble. When they finished chess they inspected the Recent Returns shelf to see what other people had been reading lately, and to try to guess what sort of person had taken out the books.

'*To the Lighthouse*,' Mandy read out. 'Maybe Mr Drake just brought that one back. He's probably planning to go to some place like that for his holiday. He wouldn't have to listen to any skateboards round a lighthouse.'

Irene found a book called *Speaking Successfully in Public*. She grabbed it and opened it to chapter one. 'A boring speaker cannot expect people to remain seated while he/she assails them with vague waffle and badly prepared material,' she read aloud. 'If you do not win your audience in the first sixty seconds, you have *failed*.' She hastily put the book back, as though it were a stinging nettle.

'I just thought of an easy way to give that talk,' said Splinter. 'What you do tonight is practise reading print upside down. Then tomorrow just show those pictures of shields to the grade, and read out what's written under them. If you put in a lot of expression Mr Acland won't know.'

Irene looked very relieved, and while they walked back to the flats, she practised. She held the heraldry book open on her stomach, and Con and Mandy and Splinter walked backwards being an audience.

'Twelve quarters,' Irene read. 'Or separate coats of arms. The first shield occupies the dexter chief. Argent: a fesse sable between four apples gule, leaves vert. Ermine, three bows bent and stringed, palewise in fesse, gules. Sable, goutte d'or, in base an embattled wall; thereon an eagle with wings displayed, both or.'

When she finished she could tell by her audience's faces that she hadn't won them in the first sixty seconds. Splinter said that his Uncle Mac had one of those, but its radiator blew up. And because Irene was looking so depressed again, Mandy invited her to dinner. Irene ran up to her flat to ask her grandma if she could. (That was one good thing about the flats; it was handy for messages.) Then she came downstairs, tiptoeing, remembering to be quiet because of Mrs Cooper and Mr Felsenthal and Mrs Carinani. (That was a bad thing about the flats; you couldn't run messages normally and cheerfully. Instead you had to pussyfoot around a lot of other people's lives and feelings.)

Four

Mandy's mother had gone to a hairdressers' convention. She had left some barbecue chops and salad in the fridge. But Mandy was opening every cupboard door, inspecting the groceries and vegetables.

'I'm not very hungry,' said Irene. 'I won't be able to eat very much, not with that speech tomorrow. A glass of milk and a slice of tomato will do.'

'You have to eat a balanced meal to keep up your strength,' Mandy said. 'I always do, even when Mum's working late. I think I might make my speciality tonight.'

'If it's those curried marmalade

sandwiches with peanut butter topping, I don't think I want any. Last time Grandma had to give me some fruit salts.'

'That was my speciality *ages* ago,' said Mandy. 'I've developed a new one now.'

Mandy's speciality was this: she put a knob of butter in a pan over a low heat and fried two rashers of bacon. She pushed them to one side and fried a sliced tomato and sliced onion, half a colander of already cooked macaroni, and some cream of asparagus soup.

'It smells OK,' Irene said politely.

Mandy added a green paprika, cut up finely. Then she put in a sliced boiled egg, some sliced cabana sausage, and a cup of rice bubbles.

'It smells great,' said Irene. 'The pan's getting a bit full, though.'

'Room for some baked beans,' said Mandy. 'And my finishing touch, which makes it into a speciality.' She took two slices of very old, very hard rye bread out of the bread bin. The bread was difficult to cut, but she sawed it into cubes and stirred them in with the other ingredients. 'Rye bread's got more flavour if it's over ten days old,' she said. 'There, it's ready! We'll use the good green dinner plates and the red table-cloth.' The meal was interesting, because there were lots of colourful things to poke around with your fork. 'In my opinion, most food is boring,' said Mandy. 'Only two veggies and some meat. But with this, you don't need to have the TV on, even. There's enough to look at right there on your plate. Would you like some strawberry-flavoured milk to go with it?'

Irene made a strangled, yelping noise, but it wasn't because of Mandy's colour scheme. It was because she had bitten hard on one of the cubes of ten-day-old bread and wrecked her tooth brace. It wasn't a conventional break, either. The wire band had flipped down and inwards at a peculiar angle, and pinned her tongue firmly underneath. As she couldn't talk,

Mandy fetched a biro and some paper, and Irene communicated by writing. The first thing she wrote was, 'Grandma will be very upset. This brace cost as much as a new automatic washing machine.'

Mandy looked in her mouth with a large powerful torch. 'It's not so bad,' she said. 'It didn't snap. It's just bent out of shape. I can easily fix it with the pliers and some resin glue.'

'I don't think you'd better touch it,' Irene wrote. 'If it cost as much as an automatic washer it's probably made of valuable metal, like uranium. You'd better leave it for the dentist.' She looked suddenly cheerful, for the first time that day. She added a PS in happy writing that skittered all over the page like a kitten playing with a thimble: 'I won't be able to give that lecture tomorrow!'

'Then I will,' said Mandy. 'My name's next on Mr A's list.'

And that was how Mandy came to learn such a lot about castles in one night.

Five

Irene had a very nice time in the city next day. The orthodontist wasn't pleased, of course, that his skilled work had been sabotaged by a hard bit of rye bread that should have been thrown away and not kept for gourmet cooking. But after that, Irene had a lovely time shopping with her grandma, who was placid and kind and never in a hurry. She let Irene try on grown-up ladies' fur coats in posh shops and didn't take any notice of the saleswomen's snooty looks. And she let Irene stop and look at every earring on every display they passed. Irene was too scared to have her ears pierced, but she liked looking at all the different earrings, in readiness for the day when Mandy would have nagged and scolded and bossed her into the necessary courage.

When they came back from the city, Irene's grandma went to her Senior Citizens' meeting, and Mandy waited in the Beatrice Binker Reserve for Mandy and Con and Splinter to come home from school. It was much cooler there than in the flats, even if it wasn't a proper park. Next to the reserve was the site where a new service station was being built. Splinter's cousin Wayne was an apprentice bricklayer with the building firm which had the contract for the service station. Wayne's boss was called Mr O'Meara, and he was very cheerful and jokey. He wore a hankie hat with four knotted corners to keep the sun off his head. He gave Irene a whole twenty cents tip to run across to the milk bar to buy them cans of Coke. Irene bought herself an icy pole and knotted the change in a tied-up corner of her hankie.

Then she knotted the other three corners and had a hat just like Mr O'Meara. He let her put some mortar on a trowel and set two bricks.

Mandy and Con and Splinter came home from school. They went over to see why Irene had such a peculiar hat on. After they had looked at her repaired brace and the new bluebird earrings her Gran had bought even though she didn't have pierced ears yet, Mandy gave the ten minute lecture again about castles for Irene's benefit. Mr Acland had given her an A for it.

Mandy wasn't a bit shy and was very confident about giving speeches. Wayne and Mr O'Meara listened while they drank their Cokes and said that there must have been a lot of work for brickies in those medieval days, and a lot of overtime, too, if knights carried on as Mandy said they did, and went around having sieges and knocking bits out of each other's new castles.

'It must have been terrific living in a castle,' Splinter said enviously.

'If we had a bigger living-room, I'd make a model one,' said Con.

'If we had a backyard, we could make a playhouse one,' said Irene.

'We've got the Beatrice Binker Reserve and we can make a *proper* one,' said Mandy.

And that's how the castle in the Beatrice Binker Reserve started.

Six

There were a great many odds and ends lying around from the remains of the three old cottages that had been pulled down to make room for the new service station. Mr O'Meara said they could have any old junk they found, but to show him first what they were taking, in case it was Wayne's recently bought station wagon. Mandy found an old wheelbarrow full of holes and with the wheel missing. Mr O'Meara said it looked like Wayne's station wagon's gear-box, but they could take it away anyhow, and put it out of its misery.

Con Vaskelis found an old brick with a

piece out of it, like a bitten sandwich, and then he found another one with a bulge. He put them together and said, 'Hey, look, I made a wall!'

Mandy dug a hollow in the ground next to Con's two bricks and wedged the wheelbarrow in that. Then Splinter found the timber frame of a window, so they dug a little ditch with Mr O'Meara's shovel, and stuck the window frame in that. The wall grew longer.

There was a large pile of old broken bricks from the pulled-down cottages. Wayne mixed up some mortar and said the kids were pests, but they had a marvellous time sticking the old bricks together. It wasn't a very professional-looking wall. Mr O'Meara and Wayne kept looking at it and sniggering, but Mandy and Con and Irene and Splinter went on adding to it right up to dinner time. It was fascinating, making a wall.

Next day after school they found that the Council had put notices in everyone's letterboxes about the six-monthly Council clean-up, and people had been dumping all sorts of things on the roadside. (All except Mr Drake who had left for his holiday, but he never had any junk, anyhow; he never threw out anything if he could help it.) Con and Irene and Splinter and Mandy went up and down Meldrum Crescent and all the nearby streets and collected useful-looking things. They took what they collected over to the park to sort out. No one seemed to mind them going through the piles of rubbish on the roadside. They were careful not to strew everything all over the place, and they left the piles of rubbish tidier than they were in the first place.

They brought back rusted star poles, chicken wire and old chairs and boxes. They found a large dog kennel with no roof, some brooms without handles and some handles without brooms. And a kitchen stove and the door from a yellow Volkswagen and picture frames and a stack of masonite boards. And ladders with rungs missing and broken-down prams and lengths of timber and car tyres and mudguards from bikes and the drawers from a metal filing cabinet. And a huge oblong of chipboard, which they had to get Wayne to carry over the road, and a grille from a barbecue and even an old bathtub.

They added this and that to the existing wall, and it turned a corner and went right round in a semicircle and joined up again.

'Just like an Indian fort,' said Con. 'We'll need a gate.'

Someone had put one out for the Council clean up. It had *Beware Of The Dog* on it, and *No Hawkers or Canvassers, and Enter At Own Risk*. It certainly looked threatening enough to be part of a fortress. They asked for Wayne's help again. He sunk a post for them and screwed the gate hinges to that. Then he sunk another post so they would have somewhere to shut the gate and slide home its bolt, but he ran a splinter into his thumb.

'Crikey, Splinter!' he said to the real live one. 'Will you and your mates quit pestering me all the time!' But he was only crabby with pain. Mandy removed the splinter very efficiently by running over the road to her flat and bringing back an ice cube and a needle. She froze Wayne's thumb and he didn't feel a thing when she went after the splinter with the needle.

When it was nearly time to go home for tea, they stopped working and played. The wall was a marvellous thing to play in, even if it wasn't finished yet. Splinter stood outside the Enter-At-Own-Risk gate and yelled, 'Open this gate in the name of the king.'

'What king?' demanded Mandy on the other side.

'Kung Fu,' said Splinter.

'He's not kung of this place,' Mandy said, and pushed hard against her side of the gate so King Foo couldn't come in. Splinter dug his heels in and pushed from the other side. Con ran to help Mandy, and Irene ran to help Splinter. It was a brilliant, tremendous, exciting battle. Nobody won, because Irene's Grandma came to tell her that tea was ready. Splinter's mother finished her afternoon's work at the hospital canteen and came to collect Splinter to take him home and tidy him up because they were going to Splinter's cousin Cheryl's twenty-first birthday.

Splinter's mother said there was a stack of sandstone blocks that had been lying about for years in the yard behind the canteen, and they could have those blocks for their playhouse.

'It's not a playhouse,' said Splinter indignantly. 'It's a fort.' But they knew that their wall was too splendid now to be just a fort.

It was growing into a castle.

Seven

During the next weeks, no one had time to brood about how awful the flats were with no balconies and no decent backyard. They were too busy constructing a tower within the circular wall, using the sandstone blocks from the canteen yard. Wayne occasionally looked up from his work at the service station. When he couldn't bear watching their miscalculated efforts anymore, he sighed and came over to show them how to do it properly, telling them they were all nuisances. But he looked as though he enjoyed working on their castle more than the service station. He made proper foundations for the tower, and when it was high enough, he cemented an iron ladder in one wall. It hadn't started out to be a ladder. It had been a low gate which belonged to Splinter's Uncle Kevin, but Uncle Kevin had recently bought a large dog and had to replace the small gate with a high one. It made a beautiful ladder for scaling the tower to be on lookout duty.

'Give the cement a chance to set before you go shinning up it,' Wayne said. 'Now, are you sure there isn't anything else you'd like me to do?' He meant it sarcastically, but when Mandy suggested battlements for the tower, he looked quite interested, and began to line bricks up in battlement patterns.

Mr O'Meara looked over to see why Wayne had vanished instead of helping him finish the last bits of the service station. 'Oy, Wayne!' he said. 'I hope you know you're not covered by workers' compensation with that fly-by-night building firm over that side.' But he didn't

sound annoyed.

Wayne spent a lot of time getting the bricks spaced exactly right for the battlements. Mandy thought privately that he even carried on just like a little kid guarding a sandcastle when she or Con or Splinter or Irene tried to offer suggestions. But when he'd finished, everyone looked at the tower and agreed that Wayne deserved to win the Apprentice of the Year award.

'Now it's turned into a proper castle with battlements, we'll have to have a moat,' said Irene, who had willingly learned quite a lot about castles from the library books now that she was safe from having to give a ten minute lecture. They borrowed the shovel from Mr O'Meara and everyone took turns digging a moat.

'Hey, I just thought of something!' Con said, 'Are we allowed to dig up this park?'

'It's not hurting anyone,' said Mandy. 'They never come and fix up this park, anyhow. No one ever uses this park or cares about it except us.'

'No one cares except us,' said everyone and nodded righteously under their knotted handkerchief hats.

The moat started off by being only as deep as a sock, but they liked pick and shovel work so much that it grew as deep as a pair of jeans over the next few days. A tip truck came to deliver a load of pine bark to the service station for an ornamental garden. Mr O'Meara let them have some of the pine bark to stamp into the moat to make a hard floor.

'Now we have a moat and a tower with battlements, but we still need a dungeon,' said Mandy.

Wayne stuck his head over the fence and so did Mr O'Meara, and they both said the same thing in loud strict voices: *'Oy! No dungeons or tunnels!'*

Everyone looked disappointed.

'Too many accidents, kids making tunnels. The walls could cave in on you,' said Mr O'Meara. 'But, tell you what, young Wayne will stay on after work in his own time and make a proper dungeon.'

'Who, me?' said Wayne, glaring, but Mandy and Irene and Splinter and Con looked so overjoyed that he did stay back. He made a tiny, perfect concrete dungeon for the castle in the Beatrice Binker Reserve. It had two steps leading down into it, and a grille door that was part of Splinter's Aunty Bev's dismantled aviary. Everyone was allowed to press their handprints in the concrete walls while it was drying so people in the future would have a record of the original builders of the castle. Over Wayne's handprints Mandy scratched with a stick, 'Wayne, Apprentice of the Year'. That was what Mr O'Meara was always calling him when he mislaid tools or asked if he could leave early because he had a date.

Splinter had a tremendous padlock on a stout chain. It had belonged to his grandad who kept greyhounds and needed strong locks like that on his property because the greyhounds were valuable. The padlock looked absolutely right and medieval for the dungeon door.

Once the concrete had set, the dungeon was used as a storehouse for lunches on weekends, and the library books about heraldry and castles which they kept renewing, and for storing Irene's budgie's spare packet of seed. They sometimes brought the budgie in its cage over to the castle. Con painted out all the letters except *Hawk* in the *No Hawkers or*

Canvassers sign and they hung the cage next to that. A hawk was a suitable thing to have at a castle, even if their one was slightly on the small side and bright yellow.

Eight

One rainy Sunday afternoon they all made a flag in Mandy's living room. The flag was the roof section of a small tent which had belonged to Splinter's big sister Carol when she had been interested in Guides and camping. Now she was more interested in jazz ballet and ten pin bowling, and she said Splinter could have that old tent.

They spread the piece of tent out on the floor and trimmed off all the uneven edges. Then Con, who was very good at sketching as well as chess, outlined the figure of a lion with a felt pen. The lion had his mouth open ready for roaring, both front paws held up, and his tail held at a proud angle. Mandy said it was a lion rampant, which was medieval for 'Look out!' She said it in a casual, off-hand voice, but she was really showing off as she'd only that minute read it in the library book about heraldry while they were deciding what to paint on their flag.

Irene's grandma had given them a tin half full of yellow paint and they filled in Con's outline lavishly then waited for it to dry. They waited ten minutes and Mandy tested the lion's rampant paws and had to go upstairs and borrow some turps as well from Irene's grandma. So they played a game of each sucking half a lemon and seeing who could keep their face expressionless the longest, and then tested the paint again. It was still wet, so they checked the tin label, which said twenty-four hours because it was enamel paint. But it was worth waiting for.

Next afternoon the dry lion looked absolutely stupendous and truly rampant.

45

Splinter's big brother, Russell, was the coach of the local football team, and he let them have a length of broken goal post (the upper, skinnier part) to use as a flag pole. They tied on the flag, stuck the pole in the tower floor and shored it up with bricks and dirt. Then they stood back and looked up.

A little wind scampered across the park and nudged the flag, and the lion stirred. The wind tugged harder and the lion stretched out to his full length. You could almost believe that the Beatrice Binker Reserve was filled with the sound of roaring.

Then everyone began to make swords. Splinter's little nephew, Trent, had a handsome plastic sword, and next time Splinter was over at his place, he swapped Trent a matchbox car collection for the sword and brought it along to the castle. Everyone else looked at the cardboard cylinders from kitchen plastic wrapping, or the umbrellas they had been using, and decided that their swords were a disgrace to the castle and the lion. So they asked the carpenter who was doing the inside of the service station if they could use some of his off-cuts. He not only said yes, but nailed cross-bars to the offcuts for them.

Mandy took her wooden sword home and bound the hilt with red velvet. She sewed on gold and silver and green glass buttons which looked just like precious jewels. Then she sprayed the blade with gold paint. That sword looked so grand that they kept it to make knights out of people by tapping them on the shoulders, as kings and queens did in the olden days.

Everyone wanted to be a knight.

'We can't *all* be,' said Mandy. 'There has to be ordinary soldiers and pages and cooks. And they probably had someone to clean out the moat.'

'And people who knitted the knights' armour,' said Irene stubbornly.

'And prisoners in the dungeon,' said

Mandy, frowning at her.

But no one, not even Mandy, wanted to be a cook when there was a battle going on, with an army trying to swarm across the moat and invade the castle and capture the lion flag. They all took turns at being the invaders or the defenders, but it was fantastic, no matter which side you belonged to.

And then a real battle started!

Mr Drake came back from his holiday on a Saturday morning. His car was just as clean as it had been when he left Meldrum Crescent, and he didn't have any of the things that people usually bring back from their vacation, such as sunburn, or car stickers, or frivolous shirts with palm trees and pictures of hula girls printed on them.

Irene was sitting on the castle battlements trying to knit a suit of chain mail armour. She had a reel of eighteen gauge copper wire, and she had cast some big loopy stitches on to a curtain rod, and was trying to finger-knit them evenly. All her fingers were wearing band-aids.

Mandy and Con and Splinter were trying to nail a tapestry up above the castle door. The tapestry unfortunately didn't have unicorns or deer-hunting or falcons embroidered on it. In fact it was an abstract design in purple and orange synthetic yarns, but Splinter's Aunty Raelene had found that it clashed with her living room curtains, so she let Splinter have it. Mandy nailed one side of the tapestry to the door frame and held up the other while Con and Splinter stood back and looked at the effect. They decided that she must have put it upside down, so Mandy was having to prise out the nails and begin again.

When Mr Drake got out of his neat grey car, the children became noticeably less relaxed. Irene concentrated fiercely on her metal knitting, as though there really was a very cross knight shivering in his singlet downstairs saying, 'Make haste, wench, 'tis bitter cold.'

Mr Drake began to unload some of his
luggage. He hadn't taken away any
normal holiday gear, such as a fishing line
or a camera. Instead he had taken a lot of
account ledgers and an umbrella, as
though he had expected the weather to be
nasty. He took them inside his house and
when he came out he glanced over at the
reserve and saw the castle.

50

'I don't think he likes castles as much as we do,' said Con apprehensively.

Mr Drake apparently didn't like them at all. He marched across the road and into the reserve. 'Who put up this pile of old rubbish?' he demanded. 'It's an outrageous eyesore!'

The children didn't think their castle was an eyesore. 'We've been told it's stupendous,' they said, truthfully, for they had all told each other that.

'It's sheer vandalism on the part of someone,' said Mr Drake. 'I'm going to write a letter to the editor of the *Meldrum Gazette*. Just as soon as I unpack my raincoat, my first-aid box and my electric blanket.'

When he had gone away to do that, Irene said in a scared voice, 'We should have told him it was us who put all this stuff in the Beatrice Binker Reserve. Why didn't we?'

'He didn't give us a chance to,' said Splinter. 'He always carries on like . . .

what was the name of that siege weapon in the library book?'

'A battering-ram,' said Con. 'Anyhow, he'd never write to the *Meldrum Gazette.*'

But Mr Drake certainly did.

When the *Meldrum Gazette* came out on Wednesday, they had the first copy in Meldrum Crescent because of Splinter's paper round. The ink was still moist from the press, and the paper smelled rich and fresh and nearly good enough to eat. But right there on the Letters to the Editor page was Mr Drake's letter, as truculent as could be.

'Sir', ('He didn't even write "dear",' said Irene.)

'Are you aware that a pile of old rubbish and junk has been dumped recently in the Beatrice Binker Reserve? It constitutes a health hazard and a complete lack of civic pride. Something should be done about it immediately. The Beatrice Binker Reserve is a memorial park, and the Council should see that it is kept impeccably tidy at all times. I wish to see this abhorrence removed immediately. Henry Drake, rate-payer.'

'What's an abhorrence?' asked Irene nervously. Splinter said that his mum had a touch of that when she had her wisdom tooth out, but a shot of penicillin had fixed it up.

Mr Drake came out to his letter-box to get his copy of the *Gazette*. 'What sort of paper boy do you call yourself, eh?' he said sternly to Splinter. 'You left this paper jutting out of the back of my box by several inches. I've got a good mind to go round to the newsagency and complain.'

'Last time you told me not to leave it poking out the front because it wasn't in line with the fence,' Splinter said. 'Your box is the wrong size, Mr Drake. I've got to leave the paper sticking out one side or the other.'

'Stuff and nonsense,' said Mr Drake. 'Papers can be folded to fit any space. That's the fault of modern-day children;

none of you will take the time to do a good, honest job.'

Mandy waited for him to finish telling Splinter off, then she held out their copy of the *Meldrum Gazette*, opened at the Letters to the Editor page. The print in Mr Drake's letter looked like an angry swarm of biting, stinging insects. 'About this letter,' she said. 'It's not really a pile of junk over there in the park. I mean, it started off as junk from the Council clean-up campaign, but it's in a sort of order now. It's nice, really, when you get up close. We put it there. It's our castle.'

'Want to come over and have a proper look?' asked Con. 'We'll be glad to show you around.'

'Do you mean to tell me that you kids dumped that rubbish there just to play some stupid game?' demanded Mr Drake. 'How dare you take away rubbish belonging to the Council collection! You just wait till the Council catches up with you! Someone will turn up, soon as they read my letter in the *Gazette,* and they'll load all that junk into a truck and cart it off to the tip where it belongs. Cluttering up a memorial park indeed! You ought to be ashamed!' And he went inside his house and snapped the door shut like a cuckoo popping back into its clock.

Mandy and Irene and Splinter and Con retreated to the castle. They didn't feel very much like playing, but Mandy took her helmet down from its hook and set it on her head. She tried to imagine that it was a piece of real armour that could withstand any blow.

They kept all their helmets by the drawbridge, where they could be easily reached in case a battle started. Mandy's helmet was a short wig her mother had used ages ago when she was a hairdressing apprentice. Mandy had accidentally fused all its nylon curls together into a tight mesh when she was trying to invent an instamatic permanent wave machine from the steam iron. Con's was a punctured football dented into a skull shape. Irene's was a silver lamé turban which had probably been quite elegant when her grandma had worn it in the 1940s. Splinter had an old crash helmet, which would have looked better with a plume.

'I think we should all get plumes for our helmets,' said Mandy. 'Splinter, have you got any relations who keep chickens?'

'Probably,' said Splinter. 'It's hard work keeping track.'

Nine

Next door, Mr O'Meara and Wayne were packing their equipment in the van and getting ready to leave. They'd finished all the bricklaying work at the service station. Mr O'Meara called them over and showed them where he had left a pile of bits and pieces they could have, in case they ever wanted to extend their castle. Mandy gave Mr O'Meara the thank-you gift they'd all bought with their pocket money. It was a packet of colourful king-sized handkerchiefs, which would knot up beautifully into hankie hats. For Wayne they had something he could use in his station wagon. It was a lambswool seat cover they had found during the Council clean-up. They had washed it carefully by hand in several different lots of water, and dried it with a hair dryer, and then teased out all the matted wool so that it looked as though it belonged in a spring meadow fragrant with clover and bees.

Wayne and Mr O'Meara were very touched by the farewell presents. Wayne put his lambswool cover on the front passenger seat because he said it was too classy to sit on in overalls. He said that if the castle ever got knocked about in a siege, to contact him through Splinter, and he'd come and attend to the repairs.

'We might just be having a proper siege,' Mandy said, and showed Mr O'Meara the newspaper letter.

'Phooey,' Mr O'Meara said when he read it. 'Who's going to take any notice of a letter in the *Meldrum Gazette*? Goes round fish and chips, that's all that little paper does. I wouldn't worry, sweetheart.' He sounded very cheerful and easy as he got into his van. 'If Mr Drake comes over here moaning and carrying on, you just bung him in the dungeon,' he said and he drove away down Meldrum Crescent after Wayne's station wagon.

Mandy watched them go. She had a panicky sensation, as though she were the commander of an army, and half her troops, the half that drove the tanks and manned the heavy artillery, had all deserted.

She looked across the road and saw Mr Drake walking around inspecting his garden. His face didn't register any of the feelings people usually experience when they are looking at lovely summer annuals. It remained sharp and grim and full of dour authority.

Mandy felt cold suddenly, in spite of the summer. She walked casually into the castle after Con and Irene and Splinter, but when she was inside, she quickly pulled up the drawbridge and fastened it.

Ten

Mr O'Meara was right. Nobody seemed to take any notice of the letter in the *Gazette*. No one from the Council arrived to inspect the castle in the Beatrice Binker Reserve. Con went ahead making a portcullis from an old banana lounge, which was lowered from the tower on strong ropes made of plaited pantyhose. It was meant to be only a temporary portcullis until Splinter managed to track down a cattle grid amongst his relatives.

Mr Drake came barging across the street. 'Bringing more junk in here, are you?' he asked angrily. 'Right, then. If the people on the Council don't bother to read the local paper, they'll get something stronger. I'm going to get up a petition and have it signed by all the rate-payers. Let's see the Council ignore something like that! They'll send round a truck to cart off this rubbish quicker than you can say Beatrice Binker Reserve!'

He began right away. He clipped an impressive stack of paper to a clipboard and tied on a biro with a string, as though he suspected that people might sign and quickly shut their doors and laugh through the keyholes because they had his biro and wouldn't give it back.

Then he went around all the houses in the streets near the Beatrice Binker Reserve. Most people hadn't even noticed the little castle, but when Mr Drake told them in his battering-ram voice that there was an abhorrence in the neighbourhood park, and showed them his newspaper letter, a lot of them said anxiously, 'Really? Fancy that!' and signed his petition.

When he finished, he posted it in the

letterbox outside the reserve. The enormous envelope was obviously crammed to bursting with signatures. 'Only a matter of time, now,' Mr Drake said, smirking with triumph over the fence. 'I should imagine that you'll all get into a great deal of official trouble!'

Official trouble sounded much worse than the other kind.

'We can make a petition, too,' Mandy whispered to Con and Irene and Splinter. They went back to the flats to search for paper and an envelope. Mandy's mother's writing paper was perfumed and decorated with little red hearts. It seemed a bit light-hearted for such a serious thing as a petition. Irene had some stationery with pictures of tabby cats all over it, which wasn't suitable, either, but her grandma gave them some plain sheets of paper and a long envelope.

Writing the letter was much harder than finding the paper and envelope. As each sentence was organised, Mandy wrote it down in her best handwriting. This is what it looked like:

Please sign this and help us keep our castle we made in the Beatrice Binker Reserve. It took ages to make. It's the best place of anywhere to play round here. You should see the dungeon. We are always very careful to pick up our orange peel and papers and put them in the bin. So it is not a health hazard. The castle has been put together using a very good brand of cement. Also, we have thousands of good ideas to make the castle even nicer when we have enough pocket money saved.

They tried to think of some.

'We could have pot plants along the battlements,' said Irene. 'And make some curtains for the windows. Grandma has a nice pink floral dressing gown she doesn't wear anymore.'

'Pink floral curtains would look terrible in a castle,' Splinter said.

'We could maybe make a big screen like that one at school when we have films,' said Con. 'Only it'd have to be a lot bigger. We could stick grass all over it with glue and keep it pulled down in front of the castle. Mr Drake couldn't say the castle's an eyesore if it's kept covered up.'

So Mandy wrote that down because they all thought it was brilliant. They didn't have a clipboard, so they sticky-taped the sheets of paper to Irene's grandma's pastry board. Grandma signed the petition, but although she was so sweet natured, she didn't really understand about the castle. Irene tried to explain about Mr Drake and what the castle meant to them, but her gran said vaguely, 'I would have thought they'd be very pleased with you kiddies collecting all that rubbish and stacking it neatly in the park out of the way. Some people just grow up with a mouth full of vinegar and lemon. I wouldn't take any notice of that sour old Mr Drake if I was you.'

They combed their hair with their fingers to look respectable, and Mandy made Splinter take off his brother Chad's black T-shirt, which had 'Northside Sharpies' written on the front with fluorescent paint. Then they went up and down the street trying to find people willing to sign *their* petition to the Council. It was an unfortunate time to choose. That afternoon, after Mr Drake had finished knocking on all the doors, Meldrum had been overrun by people calling at houses for various things. There had been high school and technical college students wanting sponsors for a Ping Pongathon, and a Scone Bakathon. There had been someone collecting donations for a hospital, someone selling cosmetics, and someone doing a market survey on coffee brands. And everyone was tetchily fed up with being summoned to their front door.

The lady at the first house where they called didn't even bother to read their petition. 'What castle?' she said impatiently. 'Everyone's nattering on about castles today. I don't know anything

about castles. Cream brick veneer is good
enough for me!' and she shut the door in
their faces.

'I can't afford to sponsor any more kids
for walkathons or pancake eatathons or
whatever,' the lady at the next house said,
and she turned on her vacuum cleaner
before Mandy could say one word.

One man did read their petition right
through, but he growled. 'You kids have
got a nerve! Cramming up land that
doesn't even belong to you with junk!'

'Beatrice Binker, whoever she was, wouldn't mind,' said Mandy. 'She meant that little park to be used, otherwise she wouldn't have given it to the Council. And we're the only ones who ever use it. And junk's not junk when it's been recycled.'

'Don't give cheek,' the man said sternly, though Mandy hadn't been at all. 'Anyhow, I signed one letter today about castles. A whole bunch of other people had their names down, all rate-payers. And it was run properly, that other petition, by someone who knew what he was talking about. Mr Drake, that's who. Shut the gate after you as you go.'

It was just about the same at every house they visited. Their petition to the Council didn't look very impressive. When it grew dark and everyone had to go back to the flats, Splinter was in charge of posting the petition first thing in the morning. He cheated a bit by getting his little brother Dominic to sign, even though Dominic didn't go to school yet. Splinter guided his writing hand. Dominic grew enthusiastic and drew a great big wobbling helicopter right across the letter before Splinter could stop him. And purple texta colour doesn't rub out. Splinter put the petition in his shirt pocket ready to post first thing. But while he was asleep, his mother put his shirt through the washing machine.

Next morning Mandy tried to resurrect the petition by spreading it out in the sun. 'Maybe we could fray the edges some more and stick on a red seal,' she said gloomily, 'like a medieval letter. It would look a bit different, I suppose, from the ones the Council usually get.'

But when the petition dried, the only decipherable thing on it was the outline of Dominic's helicopter. So they didn't post it.

But Mr Drake's petition reached the Council. Two days later a car with the Meldrum city coat of arms ('Sable, one etoile argent, and a funny looking sheep with a belt round its middle,' Mandy said knowledgeably) drove down the crescent and stopped outside the Beatrice Binker Reserve.

The driver got out and advanced to the drawbridge. 'Look here, you kids,' he said. 'You just can't go round putting up buildings without a permit. Not here in this park. You have to have a thing called a Building Permit. I'm really sorry, I can see you must have a great time playing in this Indian fort . . .'

'Castle,' said Mandy, Con, Irene and Splinter.

' . . . but it's upsetting a lot of people who live round here. We got a signed petition in the mail. They claim that your stockade is detracting from the value of their properties. If we get a complaint like that from the rate-payers, we have to investigate. I'm sorry kids, but we'll have to send someone along tomorrow to take all this stuff down. Three p.m. tomorrow, sharp, we've promised the organiser of this petition. In future, if you want to build an air raid shelter . . .'

'Castle!' said Irene and Con and Splinter and Mandy.

' . . . you'd better ask your dads to knock one up in your backyard for you.'

'We haven't got a dad,' said Mandy and Irene.

'And we haven't got a backyard,' said Con and Splinter.

But the inspector wasn't listening. He crossed that particular job off the list in his notebook and got back into his car and drove away. It seemed incredible that a scribbled note in a little book had the power to topple a castle.

Eleven

The flag on the castle tower wasn't fluttering. There was no wind, so it hung straight down, heavy and sad, and the lion looked like it was sleeping. Or dead.

Irene felt like crying when she looked up at that still banner.

'They didn't sit around bawling in the olden days when they saw the enemy charging up the hill,' said Mandy. 'They *did* things. So we will, too. Maybe we could get a television channel to come out here and take a film of our castle. The Peter Beale Show, something like that. If it was on the Peter Beale Show, I bet the Council wouldn't dare pull our castle down. It

71

would be too famous.'

'The Peter Beale Show wouldn't send a camera out here,' said Splinter. 'They only do big important things on that programme. Like racehorses getting nobbled.'

'The castle is important,' said Mandy.

'Mr Drake doesn't reckon it is.'

'Mr Drake and the Council are big and important,' said Irene miserably and they all fell silent.

'They didn't hang round being silent in the olden days,' Mandy said. 'Not with arrows whizzing past their heads. They used to treat it as an emergency.'

Splinter had some emergency money in his jeans. His mother made him carry it around for when he was out on his paper round. She worried that he might skid on the wet road and break his leg. The money was for him to ring up the nearest one of his relations to come and take him to hospital.

They all crammed into the phone box

outside the milk bar and hunted through the directory for the number of Peter Beale's television station. Mandy said she guessed it would be under C for Channel, and Splinter said it wouldn't, it would be under T for TV.

'Could I please speak to Mr Beale if he's not interviewing anyone?' Mandy said nervously into the phone when they did find the number. Mr Beale's show was on every week night, and it seemed a terrible cheek on their part to ask to speak to anyone so famous. Maybe the lady on the TV switchboard thought so, too, because she said they must send in a letter if they wanted Mr Beale to investigate anything.

'It has to be something really important to get into the Peter Beale Show,' she said, sounding polite, but very busy. 'Did you say it was about play equipment in some park? And someone was wanting to replace it?'

Mandy tried hard to explain about the little castle in the Beatrice Binker Reserve.

'We started off with these two bricks,' she babbled, because she was feeling so distraught. 'And we'd read about castles for Irene's speech, only I had to give that, because her tongue was stuck under the tooth brace . . .' She could see the castle across the street, and while she watched, the flag stirred briefly, as though the lion knew about their efforts to save the castle, and was taking heart. 'And then we found this old wheelbarrow, and all sorts of other things to make the wall bigger. And Wayne, that's Splinter's cousin, did some concreting for us . . .'

'Pardon, dear?' said the secretary. 'This line is very bad. Why don't you get your mother to write it all in letter form and send it in to us, and if Mr Beale thinks he can use it as a suitable news story, we'll be in touch.'

'There's nowhere else to play,' Mandy said desperately. 'And we worked so hard. It's not an eyesore. I'm looking at it right now, and it's lovely. It's only a little castle, and it doesn't take up all that much space. Splinter has an Uncle Denny in the fire brigade, and we might be getting a real brass helmet. It's just not fair. I bet Beatrice Binker wouldn't mind if we made a castle in her park . . .'

'I'll take down the name of the street, and I'll see that a memo gets to the producer. Meldrum Crescent, is it? But I really don't want to get your hopes up for nothing, dear,' said the receptionist. 'You must realise that we can't cover every little story that comes in.' She didn't quite hang up in Mandy's ear, but it was only a mouse whisker twitch away from it.

Mandy could hardly see the castle because her eyes were blurry and damp. She blinked angrily (for she was always telling Irene off for not having better control over her tear ducts) and the Beatrice Binker Reserve swam back into focus. 'I don't think they're going to bother,' she said when she thought she could trust her voice not to wobble. 'So there's only going to be us to stick up for the castle. Just as well it's a school holiday tomorrow. We've got to be here for the siege.'

Twelve

They got up early next day to prepare for the siege.

'Food's important,' said Mandy. 'Sometimes they even had to eat their horses in the olden days. That's if the people outside stayed on for months and tried to starve them out.'

'I don't think Grandma would let me stay over in the castle that long,' said Irene doubtfully. 'I don't think she'd even let me stay overnight.'

'I don't think the Council would send anyone after five,' said Mandy. 'It would cost them too much in wages. People get time and a half for working out of business hours. We've got to be prepared for anything, though.'

They packed Irene's grandma's shopping trolley with supplies of food: cans of alphabet spaghetti in tomato sauce; a large packet of corn flakes; a tin of sardines; cheese cracker biscuits, and a tin of peaches in syrup. And a tin opener. While they were pushing the trolley past the fruit shop, the man who owned it gave them a bag of free cooking apples. The apples were really only fit for guinea pigs, but if you cut out the brown bits, they were nearly as good as new. 'Better than dead horses, anyway,' said Irene.

After they had stored all the food in the tower, Con went back to the flats and brought along six two-litre milk cartons filled with lemon cordial.

'It's a pity this castle hasn't got a well,' said Mandy. 'We're going to be in trouble when we've drunk all that up. Thirst is worse than starvation.'

Splinter went and borrowed a hose from

the people in the ground floor flat and connected it to the park tap. The nozzle of the hose just reached to the tower window. Everyone thought Splinter was brilliant for finding the means of connecting the castle to the city water mains. 'Not all that brilliant,' said Con. 'Mr Drake and the Council can just turn off that tap.'

So Mandy made an emergency vacuum flask of her new speciality, which was a very complicated eggnog drink. She was intending to develop and market it one day as a high-energy food for astronauts. It didn't taste very nice because the special ingredient was camomile.

'I'm just going back to the flat to get my air mattress,' said Irene.

'They didn't bother about air mattresses in castle sieges in the olden days,' Mandy said sternly.

'They would have if they'd been invented then,' said Irene, who liked to be comfortable. She went back to her flat and fetched the mattress and her quilt and pillow as well, and her bean-bag chair. And her chain armour knitting, which was still only into its second painful row.

After they were all in the castle, Mandy drew up the drawbridge, then she let down the banana lounge portcullis, then she shut the castle door and fastened it. 'Now,' she said. 'All we have to do is wait for the bulldozers.'

Everyone went very quiet, as they all thought privately about bulldozers. Suddenly the little castle in the Beatrice Binker Reserve seemed very small and vulnerable.

Thirteen

But the Council didn't send along a
bulldozer. What happened was that
one man all by himself came at three p.m.
in a Council truck. He even had very
nice manners for an invading army.
He said he was sorry that the Council had
sent him along to do that job. 'I really am
sorry, kids,' he told them. 'But you'll have
to nip out of there, now. I've got to start
taking this tree-house or whatever it is
down.'

'It's a *castle*,' said Mandy. 'And if you
lay a finger on it, we'll defend it to the
death.'

Mr Drake, who had been watching for

the Council to arrive, hurried over to the park to make sure the man in the truck did the job properly.

'Come on, you get out of there when you're told,' he ordered Mandy and Irene and Con and Splinter. 'Cheeky little brats. Kids these days are all the same. Too darn smart for their own good.'

'If you come any closer, Mr Drake,' Mandy said, 'we're going to have to throw boiling oil over the battlements.'

Mr Drake was startled and indignant at such a threat. He jumped down into the moat and rattled the closed drawbridge, so Mandy gave the order for boiling oil to be thrown, only of course it wasn't boiling oil really, it was two litres of lemon-flavoured cordial. Mr Drake made as much fuss as if it had been boiling oil. He told Mandy he was going to her flat to complain to her mother.

'My mum's at work, and she has a perm, two tints and a bride's blow wave to do today,' said Mandy, 'so she won't be home for ages.'

The Council man scolded them for tipping lemon cordial over Mr Drake. He took some tools out of his truck and used one of them to try to lever the drawbridge down. So he had two litres of boiling oil poured over him, also.

Mrs Carinani and Mrs Palmer passed the reserve on their way home from the shops. They stopped and stared over the fence. 'Oh, look,' said Mrs Palmer. 'There's a nice little Swiss chalet thingummy in the Beatrice Binker Reserve.'

'It's a castle,' said Mandy. She was very good at public relations because she had the chance to watch how her mother dealt with clients at Madame Tanya's Beauty Salon in the city. She gave Mrs Carinani and Mrs Palmer a vivid lecture about the castle and why the man from the Council was there with his pick. 'We even tried to ring up the Peter Beale Show,' she said. 'That's how much we want to save this castle. But they didn't come out. I suppose because we didn't have a grown-up with us when we rang.'

'I always watch the Peter Beale Show,' Mrs Palmer said, enthusiastically. 'It would be marvellous to see Meldrum Crescent on the telly! Tell you what, love, I'll just nip over to the phone and give that TV station a ring. I'll tell them there's a red-hot story going begging and they'd better get out here quick smart. Fancy, I might even see myself on the telly tonight! No one go knocking any bricks down until I get a camera van out here. My word, this is more exciting than the cut-price battle at the two supermarkets!' She hurried across the street to the phone box. The man from the Council wasn't pleased.

'There wasn't any need for that,' he said to Mandy, offended. 'You kids are just making trouble.'

'You could have that pile of junk down

and cleared away before a television camera gets here, if you stopped wasting time,' Mr Drake said impatiently. 'Just get on with it. Those kids haven't got any say in the matter. The Council's ordered it to come down and that's that.'

'Hold on a minute,' said Mrs Carinani. 'It's the kids' cubby-house. Why shouldn't they have a cubby-house in the park? It's not hurting anyone. The Council's getting too big for its boots, always making people chop trees down and get rid of the chickens in their backyard. Won't be allowed to breathe, next. If you ask me, the Council ought to be dumped on a truck and carted off to the tip.'

The man from the Council looked embarrassed. 'I'm only doing a job,' he mumbled resentfully. 'Pile of junk in the middle of the Beatrice Binker Reserve, has to come down right away, protest from an important rate-payer, that's all I was told. It wasn't my idea at all. I only got sent here to do it.' He looked round at all the faces.

The crowd had grown to include some of the machinists from the Kozisnooze Slumberwear factory, who had come outside for their afternoon break.

'How about that, threatening poor little kids with a pick!' someone muttered.

'I reckon it's my afternoon tea break,' the Council man said, turning pink.

'That's right,' said Mrs Carinani. 'Knocking off time, instead of knocking down time, that's a bit more like it.'

The Council man went and shut himself up in his truck. He self-consciously began to eat a corned beef and tomato sauce sandwich. Mr Drake went over and ordered him to get out and finish the job. 'I'm not allowed to work when it's raining. Union rules,' said the man from the Council.

'It's not raining at all,' said Mr Drake.

'Rain was forecast last night. So I'm going to sit here in the old truck and see how the weather shapes up,' said the man from the Council and he wound up the window. Mr Drake thumped angrily on the glass for a while, and then he saw a police car going down Meldrum Crescent. He darted out and waved it to a stop and came back with a police constable.

Fourteen

The besieged occupants of the castle weren't scared, because they saw that it was only young Constable Mick Harrison who lived with his mother in the flat below Irene's. 'Nothing to worry about at all,' said Mandy. 'I've seen him hanging up the washing. He ran out of pegs. I had to tell him you don't peg hankies up with two pegs for each one.'

'And Grandma called him upstairs that time we thought we heard a funny noise on the roof,' said Irene. 'He didn't want to go up and look because there was a huntsman spider on the fire escape. Grandma had to take it away on a piece of newspaper.'

Constable Harrison was also very interested in Splinter's big sister Carol, so he just said mildly, 'Mandy, what's this I hear about you kids tipping lemon cordial over Mr Drake?'

Mandy was glad then it hadn't been burning oil. She told Constable Harrison all about the Council wanting to pull down the castle and how they were defending it. 'Council matter, is it?' said Mick Harrison, looking relieved. 'That's all right, then, if it's a Council matter I'm not needed here. I'll go back and check with my sergeant, but I'm sure the Council has things well in hand.'

The Council hadn't really. The man in the truck had finished his corned beef sandwich and had begun on his jam doughnut and thermos of coffee. He was reading a copy of the *Trotting Globe* spread out on the steering wheel.

'I'm sorry we can't ask you in, Constable,' said Mandy. 'The castle's closed. Any other time you could come in for a visit, but it's not possible right now.'

'Closed is it?' Mr Drake demanded. 'Constable, what are you waiting for? Surely you can effect an entrance, by force if it's necessary?'

'I reckon I'd have to have a search warrant,' Mick said. 'I'll have to go and check with my sergeant about that, too.'

'I haven't finished with you! Don't you dare drive off!' Mr Drake thundered, but Constable Mick Harrison already had.

'Oh, look!' called the Kozisnooze women at the fence. 'There's one of those telly news cars coming down Meldrum Crescent!'

The man from the Council didn't want to appear on any television screen and get all the blame. 'I'll come back tomorrow when you kids are at school and take all that junk away!' he yelled and drove his truck out through the park's other exit before the television van came through the Meldrum Crescent one.

The camera men took pictures of the castle from various angles, and a reporter climbed down into the moat to ask Mandy and Con and Irene and Splinter some questions. Mrs Carinani and Mrs Palmer and the Kozisnooze women followed her down into the moat and smiled at the camera, so they could watch themselves on TV later.

Mandy and Con and Splinter and Irene put on neat, respectable faces to show they were responsible citizens. 'This is how the castle started,' Mandy began to explain. 'Con found this brick with a dent in the top, and then he found another one with a bulge that matched, and we started to make a wall.' It was difficult to make herself heard above all the clamouring voices.

The reporter wrote things down in her notebook. 'And now the Council wants to pull the castle down?' she asked. 'Right, I've got that, but we have to see that each side gets a fair hearing in our programme.

Perhaps there's someone here from the Council, or whoever is concerned with removing the castle.'

'Mr Drake was here a minute ago,' said Splinter.

Mr Drake hadn't wanted to be interviewed or photographed at all. He thought it was an invasion of his rights to privacy as a rate-payer. As soon as he saw the TV man, he had slipped behind the castle out of sight.

Irene had carelessly left her bean-bag chair outside the back wall. Mr Drake stood on it, climbed over the wall and jumped down inside the castle where he thought he would be safe from the inquisitive television camera.

Mandy glanced down and saw him and reacted as any worthy knight would have done upon sighting an invading foe. She rushed downstairs and shoved Mr Drake into the dungeon, slammed the grille and snapped the heavy padlock shut.

Mr Drake rattled the grille and roared

but nobody heard him because of the Kozisnooze Slumberwear factory siren telling the machinists that afternoon break was over. The women had to go back to work, and the TV crew left, too, because they couldn't find anyone from the opposition to interview. Mrs Carinani and Mrs Palmer ran out after the van and followed it all the way down Meldrum Crescent. They were so excited about being film stars that they forgot all about the castle as soon as they set foot outside the Beatrice Binker Reserve.

Sixteen

So the reserve was as hushed and empty as it normally was. Con, Splinter and Irene climbed down from the battlements and looked with awe at Mr Drake in the dungeon. 'I don't think he likes being in there,' said Irene nervously. She was so alarmed by the sight of Mr Drake held captive in the dungeon that she picked up her chain mail knitting for comfort. She hooked an agitated wire loop over one finger and transferred it to the curtain rod.

'It's going to be a suit of chain mail armour,' she felt obliged to explain, because Mr Drake stopped roaring and stared at it and her with pitying disbelief.

'They certainly didn't make armour out of copper,' Mr Drake said in disgust. 'Anyone with a bit of intelligence could have worked that out. Everyone knows copper turns green in the rain.'

'This is only a rough draft for a knitting pattern,' Irene said quickly. 'When I work out how to do it with copper, I'll run up a whole suit of armour out of stainless steel or whatever they used. I've nearly finished this little copper model, anyhow,' she lied. 'This is only the pocket lining, this bit.'

Mr Drake looked as though he didn't believe her, then remembered suddenly where he was and talked in loud capital letters for a long time ending with 'OPEN THIS DOOR AND I'M GIVING YOU THREE SECONDS TO DO IT!'

Splinter and Con and Irene looked at Mandy, who wore the key on a thong round her neck, but she didn't open the door. 'Splinter's cousin Wayne made that dungeon,' she told Mr Drake. 'He might be the Apprentice of the Year and have his photo in the paper, he's so clever. Did you notice the candle-holder? We're not allowed to muck round with candles and matches, so that's why the torch is there instead. The red cellophane's to make it look more like one of those burning torches they had in the olden days.'

'If this place caves in on me, you kids

will be in serious trouble,' Mr Drake snapped.

'It won't cave in,' promised Mandy. 'That's high grade cement, that lining. Kick it as hard as you want to, it won't budge. All the castle's like that. Mr O'Meara and Wayne checked everything we put up. It's a lovely castle. Even the man from the Council didn't really want to knock it down.'

Mr Drake didn't answer. He finished kicking the walls and started on the grille door.

'That won't budge, either,' said Mandy. 'Nice thick chain and padlock, aren't they? The rest of the castle's just great, too. I don't know how people could *not* like castles. If I was a park designer, I'd build one in every park in the country. This one could be improved, of course, because we had to start from scratch. It could do with some more slit windows for arrows, and a barbican – that's a covered passage to protect the main gate, we read it in the library book. And pine bark doesn't look as good as water in a moat. But we don't mind that we haven't got all the things right off. It's just as much fun working on them. If I lived in your house, Mr Drake, I'd certainly rather look at a fantastic little castle in the Beatrice Binker Reserve than just bare grass.'

'Have you quite finished?' Mr Drake demanded fiercely.

'No,' said Mandy, 'there's another thing. We're going to have to keep you prisoner, Mr Drake, until we get reinforcements to defend the castle while we're at school tomorrow.'

Mr Drake would probably have jumped up and down with rage, but the dungeon had been designed for short people who had paper rounds and homework and swap card collections, so he couldn't do any jumping at all.

'It won't take long,' Mandy said. 'Hundreds of people watch the Peter Beale Show. Their switchboard will be jammed, like the time they said about the ten pups needing a foster mother. Tomorrow, when we have to go to school, thousands of people will be here sitting in the castle, and the man from the Council won't dare pull it down. But until all those people arrive, I'm keeping you locked up in the dungeon.'

'But Mandy, we might get into trouble, using real prisoners,' Irene said, looking very worried.

'There's no "might" about it,' said Mr Drake. 'You'll all be packed off to a home for uncontrollable children.'

'My cousin Fred was in one of those places,' Splinter said uneasily. 'He didn't like it much.'

'Neither will you,' said Mr Drake. 'And it will serve you right, making a laughing stock of the Beatrice Binker Reserve on public TV. I won't allow it.'

'Beatrice Binker, whoever she is, wouldn't mind,' Mandy said.

'You don't know anything about

Beatrice Binker,' Mr Drake said sharply.

'If she was nice enough to give this land to the Council for a park, I bet she wouldn't mind kids playing here and building things. You couldn't do a thing about it if she said we could. I just wish I knew who she is or where she lives. I'd ring up and tell *her* about the castle.'

Mr Drake went rather quiet.

'You can't ring her up,' he said at last.

'I can if I want to,' said Mandy.

'No, you can't. Beatrice Binker died forty years ago.'

'Well then, we'll just have to manage,' Mandy said. 'We've got Peter Beale and all the millions of people who'll be turning up here tomorrow. And there's no use carrying on and yelling, Mr Drake, because no one will hear you. No one ever uses this park except us. I might send you over some dinner later, but I'll have to think about it. And Splinter will deliver your paper here instead of in your letter-box. I don't know why you're looking like that, either. Prisoners in the olden days didn't ever get papers delivered to them. They were locked up for years and years and you've only been there for a few minutes. You've got the torch in there, and Con's sketch book and his felt pens, and my eggnog. No prisoner could ask for more. I'll come back and let you out as soon as we've got our reinforcement army together.'

Mr Drake's expression was as powerfully angry as a Pharaoh's curse. Mandy and Con and Splinter and Irene left the castle, closing the door behind them. Not that anyone ever went into the park except themselves, but closing the castle door was what they did every afternoon when they left. It had become a ritual, like putting a child safely to bed for the night.

Seventeen

Mr Drake listened to them depart. Then he furiously rattled the grille door till he realised it was totally useless, and that his only audience was a colony of daddy long legs spiders in a corner of the dungeon. (Splinter had brought them and their cobwebs over from the flats to make the dungeon look more authentic.)

Mr Drake stopped shaking the door and sat down to rest. He scowled at the dungeon wall where it had been signed by the original builders. Mandy had spelled 'apprentice' wrongly. Mr Drake flinched when he saw it. He couldn't bear sharing the same dungeon as a spelling error, so he picked up one of Con's felt pens and added the missing 'p'. He made a small neat arrow pointing to the space where it was supposed to fit.

It was the first time in his life he had ever written on a wall.

He sat back and looked at it, then he made a row of little feathers on the tail of the arrow with a different colour. The smooth concrete was a splendid surface to write on.

There were other things written on the walls, because anyone who was put in the dungeon as a prisoner was apt to indulge in graffiti.

'Sir Swithin, 1066,' Mr Drake read. 'King Foo was here under wrongful arrest three score years and ten.' 'Prisoners are not allowed to escape without asking first, and this means you, Splinter.' 'Sir Lancelot – conquered on Monday!' 'I was not! You cheated!' 'Falcon the Red will arise and get his revenge!' 'Irene, you are a traitor if you let prisoners out just because you feel sorry for them. Last warning.'

Mr Drake read the whole wall, and in a corner, low down, he wrote in his neat small writing, 'Henry Drake', and added the date. He looked at it with his head on one side and thoughtfully underlined it in red and added a border of yellow stars.

He remembered that never in his life had he ever written on a wall, and he hurled Con's felt pens aside impatiently. There was over an hour yet before the Peter Beale Show. He examined the hinges of the grille and tried to remember the rare movie matinees of his childhood, where heroes escaped effortlessly from dungeons. He tried to recall just how. In those films there

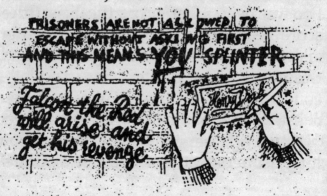

had always been guards to bribe, or a smuggled file baked in a convenient pie, or the warden's daughter would obligingly turn up at the last minute with a spare key.

He pushed against the walls, but Wayne and Mr O'Meara had done a beautiful job. There wasn't even a visible seam.

He looked at the floor. To make it more artistic and medieval, Mandy, Con, Splinter and Irene had paved it with broken concrete. Mr Drake prised up one of the pieces. 'Dig my way out and show those kids who's boss,' he thought triumphantly. He looked around for something to dig with. There wasn't anything suitable except the lid of the thermos flask, but it made quite a nice little shovel. Mr Drake was quite pleased with himself for thinking of it.

He made a tidy job of digging a tunnel. Being Mr Drake, he didn't just dump thermos lids of soil any old place, but spread them neatly on a sheet of Con's drawing paper. After five minutes he had made a hole the size of a pudding bowl, and was very proud of it. He even conceded that planning an escape was almost as challenging as balancing books at the end of a financial year, or combating aphids in roses.

He thought again of those old movie matinees, and at the back of his mind a picture took form. It was of himself, but he wasn't wearing his usual grey trousers and spotless white shirt and tie. In his mind he saw himself clad in a glittering suit of armour, and at his side hung a magnificent bejewelled sword.

But that detail was incorrect, he thought

fussily. They probably used to confiscate swords before tossing prisoners into dungeons. He subtracted the sword in his mind, but added a plumed helmet, a shield with a colourful coat of arms, and royal blood. He was Prince Henry, escaping from the castle of the Black Baron by digging an ingenious tunnel.

'Mr Drake, I brought you over some macaroni cheese,' Irene said diffidently.

Prince Henry jumped, startled, and banged his royal head on the dungeon roof. He rubbed the bump with one hand and quickly shoved the paving stone over the tunnel entrance with the other, so Irene couldn't see. He glared ferociously at her through the bars.

'Don't tell the others I brought this over for you,' Irene said. 'Mandy decided you shouldn't get anything, not even bread and water.'

Mr Drake was hungry after his digging, so he scooped up a large forkful of the macaroni cheese. There was a clink of metal. He made a porthole in the macaroni and found a little nail file.

'It was the best I could do,' Irene said tearfully. 'I know they're supposed to be baked in pies and smuggled in, but I didn't have time to bake a pie. And please don't mention to Mandy I brought you a file to escape with. I know you don't deserve it, but I just can't stand seeing prisoners in the dungeon.'

Mr Drake looked from the tiny nail file to the great thick chain on the dungeon door. He opened his mouth to say something very stinging and insulting, but Irene had fled back to the flats before Mandy found out she wasn't really putting rubbish into the bin on the landing.

Mr Drake finished the macaroni cheese and resumed digging. He dug out some more cups of soil and then struck a layer of granite-hard clay. To tunnel through that, he would have needed a pneumatic drill.

He tidied away the hole by replacing all

the soil and the paving stone, and then looked through the little barred window of the dungeon. In those old films, he remembered, prisoners often escaped through windows. They always had a loyal henchman waiting outside with a rope ladder and an extra horse.

There wasn't anything outside in the way of a horse, only Splinter, passing up the evening paper. He also had a handful of assorted keys.

'Don't tell Mandy,' said Splinter. 'She said she'd like to keep you there till you turned into a skeleton, but I reckon we'd get into too much strife if we did that. Mandy doesn't see it that way, though. She says we'd get a medal because of you being a public menace.'

'Oh, she did, did she?' Mr Drake growled.

'She's got the proper key round her neck, so there's no way I could get that. She's a better fighter than me. But one of these might fit.'

Mr Drake took the keys, but he wasn't a bit grateful. He just told Splinter what he would do to him when he got out, so Splinter didn't hang round, he scooted back to the flats. Mr Drake looked at the keys. There were school locker keys that should have been returned years ago, a delicate little filigree key from a diary, ordinary front door keys, a miniature silver key from Splinter's sister Carol's charm bracelet, and even a gold cardboard key from a twenty first birthday card.

But none of them was any use at all on the strong padlock that had once guarded valuable greyhounds.

Eighteen

Mr Drake turned his attention to the roof
of the dungeon, which was what he
should have looked at first. Wayne had
made it as a separate slab, but it fitted
so perfectly that you could hardly tell it
wasn't sealed to the walls. Mr Drake
discovered the seams. He searched the
dungeon for something to use as a lever,
trying a felt pen, but it snapped in two,
and a twenty cent coin from his coin bag.
(He never carried loose change in his
pockets in case it dragged them out of
shape. He had a special suede money
pouch with his name and address for
people to return it if it were lost, but there

was nothing about a reward.)

The coin wasn't long enough, but he had a pocket knife which his sister had given him for his last birthday. Although Mr Drake claimed he didn't celebrate birthdays and they were a lot of frivolous nonsense, she still felt obliged to give him a present. Over the years she had given him stacks of plain handkerchiefs, sombre ties and household account books, so in desperation she sent him the pocket knife. It had a lot of gadgets. As well as a little blade that couldn't even cut ice cream, there was a tiny torch whose light was too dim to even light up a matchbox, and a tin opener and compass in case you ever got lost in a supermarket.

The only reason Mr Drake kept the present was that he never ever threw anything away.

The one good thing about it was its strong little case. Mr Drake levered it under the seam and the slab moved slightly sideways. He made an opening large enough for his hands, and then pushed with his hands till the opening was large enough for the rest of him to escape.

Before escaping, he tidied the dungeon, because he couldn't bear to see any room disorderly, even a dungeon. He put the macaroni plate and fork neatly by the grille, and Con's felt pens back into their folder. Except the red one. On the wall where he'd signed his name, he added 'ESCAPED!' and looked at it, smirking with triumph. Then he climbed out of the dungeon.

Next to it was a section of a storm water pipe. Mr Drake supposed it must lead to the front door, which was the one he intended to use on his way out. He was going to march out of the castle front door and phone the television station to stop the Peter Beale Show, and then confront the parents of those hooligan children and have them sent to a reform school. It was hard to decide which to do first, both being appealing.

He stooped and looked through the pipe and saw the lower half of a ladder at the far end. He got down on his hands and knees and crawled through the pipe till he reached the ladder cemented into the tower wall.

It was the first time in his life he had ever crawled through a tunnel.

'Old junk belonging to the tip,' he muttered when he came to the ladder, but it felt firm enough, so he climbed up.

At the top was the chair that Mandy and Con and Irene and Splinter used as a throne. It was the bucket seat from an old car, set up on a stack of bricks. The bricks were covered with aluminium foil so that it looked royal. It was where the king or queen sat to make people into knights, and it was very comfortable to sit on, but not so comfortable for the knights. There wasn't anywhere for them to kneel except the top rung of the ladder, and they got sore knees because Irene was taking so long to knit the chain armour.

Mr Drake sat down on the throne to get his breath back. To his left was a metal pole that looked exactly like a fire station pole. 'Castles never had firepoles,' Mr Drake thought disagreeably. 'How could knights shimmy up and down a pole wearing uniform? Don't those kids learn anything at school?'

He shook the firepole but it was as firm as a mahogany gum. (Mr O'Meara and Wayne had tested it by sliding down before letting the children try. They tested it forty-seven times during their lunch break, and Wayne had also come back during afternoon tea break and tested it another seventeen times. Just to make sure, Mr O'Meara had stayed after work and tested it twenty times, all of which had seemed very excessive to Mandy and Splinter and Con and Irene.)

Mr Drake thought back to when he was in first grade at school. His ambition then had been to slide down the pole at the firestation, but he couldn't remember that anyone had ever taken him there. He looked carefully up at the sky to make sure no one was watching him from an aeroplane, then he took a grip with his hands and stepped out into space.

'There!' he said when he reached the bottom. 'I've done it. I've slid down a firepole.'

Next to the firepole was the door and the drawbridge. Mr Drake opened the door and fiddled with the drawbridge mechanism. The drawbridge wasn't as well built as the rest of the castle, and it made a terrible clatter and bang when it was worked. It was pulled up and down with two dog leashes. Splinter's grandad who owned the greyhounds had given them to Splinter. (Splinter had also asked for some spare dog muzzles, thinking they'd make very good helmet visors, but discovered that they'd only really be suitable for extremely thin knights with oddly shaped faces.)

Mr Drake lowered and shut the

drawbridge, and his expression showed that he didn't think much of it. 'Hinges need oiling,' he said to himself. 'That's the trouble with modern-day kids. Wouldn't even occur to them that things need oiling sometimes. No pride in their work.'

In their junk, he corrected sourly. Filling up the reserve with junk, they were. In a minute he was going to ring up Peter Beale and put him straight about a few things, and then he would go round to the flats and complain to whichever parent he could find.

But first there were the stairs.

'More death traps,' he said, as he put his foot on the first one.

But they were lovely stairs. They curved in a snail-shell spiral, and the materials that had gone into their making had come from many different places. It was amazing what you could use to make steps: railway sleepers, metal shoe scrapers, an old tin chest filled with soil and gravel so that it wouldn't cave in, a yellow sign which said *'Detour'*, broken concrete slabs from where the Board of Works had dug up the footpath, and lengths of timber. But everyone's favourite steps were the ones made from the sandstone blocks which had once formed a staircase in the old hospital. They were already faintly hollowed out from years of people's footsteps.

When Mr Drake finished climbing the stairs several times, he rather strangely went back to the dungeon. He crawled through the tunnel, climbed the ladder, sat on the throne, slid down the firepole (twenty-five times), opened and shut the drawbridge, and climbed the stairs all over again. Then he looked up at the lion flag.

It snapped above his head, fighting with a gust of wind, and the lion plunged into battle, fierce and proud.

Mr Drake stood looking up at it for a long time.

Then he went over to his house and rang up the Peter Beale Show.

Nineteen

Mandy, Con, Irene and Splinter gathered in Mandy's living room to watch the Peter Beale Show. None of them really felt like eating, and the macaroni cheese casserole Mandy's mother had left stood almost untasted on the coffee table. None of them felt much like talking, either, and when six-thirty came, they hunched tensely forward in their chairs, like people watching a vital championship match.

The castle was so important to them that they thought Peter Beale would have it as his first news story, but instead there was a lengthy boring discussion about taxation. After that there was a commercial break, and then an interview with some-one who had gone to gaol rather than pay a parking fine.

'Ours will be next,' Mandy said, but instead it was Peter Beale talking to a Cabinet Minister. That was followed by a commercial about Velvet being the softest soap.

There were five minutes left of the Peter Beale show.

'They've saved the castle till last because it's the most important,' said Mandy.

Irene had gnawed so much of her plait that she started to choke and had to be thumped on the back.

'SSSHHH!' said Mandy fiercely, but there was no need for silence because the last thing on the Peter Beale Show was an interview with a man who claimed to have seen a UFO in his market garden.

There wasn't anything at all about the castle.

Irene burst into tears.

'Maybe tomorrow night,' Con said.

'Maybe they didn't get the film ready in time.'

Mandy switched off the set. 'It will be too late tomorrow night,' she said bleakly. 'They'll have pulled down the castle while we're in school.'

She had a brief, sad vision of the little castle being torn down and loaded piece by piece into the Council truck, with no one there to defend it. Even Peter Beale hadn't thought it important enough. She wondered if real knights in olden times had felt as tired and sorrowful when they had battled against an invading army and lost. She thought of the lion flag being hauled down and carted off to the tip. It would be thrown in amongst the rubbish as though it were just a piece of old tent canvas.

'I'd better go down and let Mr Drake out,' she said. 'There's no point keeping him locked up any more. I don't suppose it really matters if it's him or the man from the Council who tears the castle down.'

'You don't have to worry about letting Mr Drake out,' said Splinter. 'He's probably found his own way out by now. He might've had a bunch of keys in his pocket and one fitted.'

'Or a nail file,' said Irene through her tears. 'He could have filed through the chain, so you don't have to go over there and get yelled at, Mandy.'

Perhaps she could rescue the lion flag and they could pull it up on the roof of the flats, Mandy thought, but felt sick at the idea of that proud lion caged amongst a clutter of television aerials and clothes hoists on the roof.

'I've got to go over to the reserve, anyhow,' she said. 'I left something there. Don't you want to come and have a last look at the castle while it's still standing?'

Irene started crying harder and said her grandma was expecting her. Splinter said he still had some papers to deliver down the opposite end of Meldrum Crescent.

Con said he had to go to his flat and help his mother.

Mandy could tell by their faces that none of them wanted to look at the castle for the last time, because it would hurt too much.

She went out into Meldrum Crescent, which was filled with soft, early evening light, but Mandy walked through it, bracing herself as though it were sleet. She stood at the gate of the Beatrice Binker Reserve and took her own, private, last, long look at the castle.

The sun shaved slivers of light from the metal in the castle walls, so that it danced and sparkled, and the flag danced, too, high above the tower. Mandy found that Irene and Con and Splinter were much wiser than she was; it really did hurt too much to bear.

As she looked, the flag was jerked abruptly away from its rippling dance, and plummeted downwards, as though someone inside the tower had cut the string.

Mandy stormed across the reserve and into the castle. 'Don't you dare touch that lion flag, Mr Drake!' she yelled, but the yell dissolved into staring silence, because Mr Drake wasn't damaging the flag at all. He was replacing the original wispy twine with a length of gleaming new white cord.

'Wanting this old pile of junk filmed on TV before it's even properly finished,' he muttered, not looking at Mandy. 'If there's going to be an eyesore in this park, it should be a decent one. I don't want the Beatrice Binker Reserve disgraced on television. It's a memorial park. They're coming out next week to make a proper film, I rang and told them. That ditch ought to be smartened up before then—'

'It's a moat,' said Mandy.

'Pink bark in a moat doesn't look right. It won't be a moat till I've concreted it, then you kids can fill it up with water. Or boiling oil. And that drawbridge – chain on a pulley is what they used, not dog leashes.'

'We didn't have anything else.'

'Plenty of old stuff in my garage. You shouldn't have any trouble building a proper drawbridge out of that, not to mention a barbican. You want to do something about the dungeon roof, too. Anyone can escape.'

'I guess we'll have to get a Building Permit if we're going to add anything,' Mandy said. 'The Council—'

'Council hasn't got any say in what goes on in the Beatrice Binker Reserve,' Mr

Drake said. 'Seeing it was I who gave it to them in the first place.'

'Who was Beatrice Binker, then?' asked Mandy curiously. 'Why did you call it that?'

Mr Drake didn't answer right away. Mandy looked at his face while she waited, and decided that it didn't really look like a fierce totem pole. It was just an ordinary face. A rather sad one, tinged with loss.

'It doesn't matter now,' Mr Drake said at last. 'It was a long time ago, anyway. I'll give you a hand tidying up that ditch. It spoils the look of this fort.'

'It's a castle,' said Mandy.

'Beatrice would have liked it,' said Mr Drake.